The Rising Rhymers

Mubble Puppy

Written and illustrated by
Andrew Buller

The wise wind whistled...

www.meettherhymers.com

www.andrewbuller.com

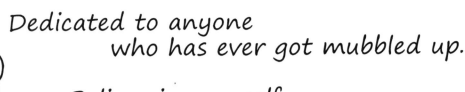

Dedicated to anyone
who has ever got mubbled up.

Believe in yourself.
Celebrate who you are.
Be amazing!

Just like Mubble Puppy.

The Rhymers series provide a wonderful way to learn through each of their fun, engaging, colourful books.

Early learning experts value the use of rhythm and rhyme in reading and language development.

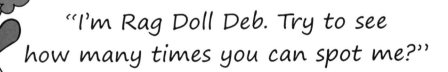

"I'm Rag Doll Deb. Try to see
how many times you can spot me?"

Andrew Buller Books

First published in Great Britain in 2016

Text & illustration copyright © 2016 Andrew Buller

I acknowledge the help of Malcolm Buller in the creative development of this story.

ISBN: 978-1535188630

Welcome

to Rhyme Island

where Rising Rhymers play and rhyme.

Things will never be the same.

It's mubble-muddle time!

Yap and Giggle tried to be quiet

at the beach

playing hide and seek.

"Hairy's coming! Hairy's coming!"

"Keep down!"

"SSSSHHHH!"

"Don't speak!"

"Boo!"

Hairy jumped!

He ran,

tripped

and landed...

SPLASH

in the sea.

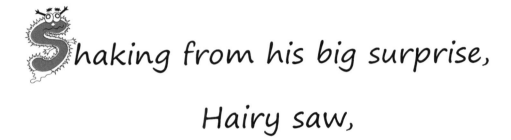haking from his big surprise,

Hairy saw,

in a basket,

two sad eyes.

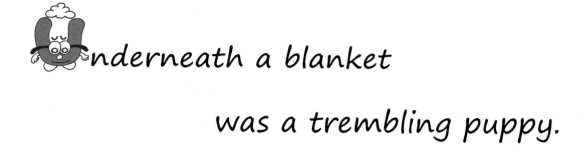nderneath a blanket

was a trembling puppy.

Hairy's arms were warm and strong.

"Come with me

to Rhyme Nursery."

"This puppy looks so poorly,

but what can we do?"

Rising Rhymers came to help

in the order they all knew.

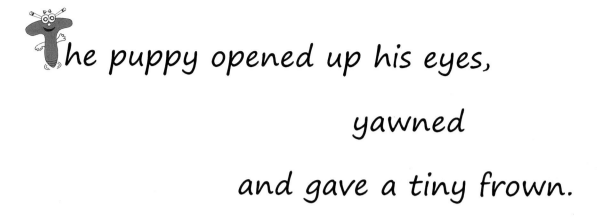The puppy opened up his eyes,

yawned

and gave a tiny frown.

He tried to climb out of his basket,

but he landed

 upside down!

"What do puppies like to eat?"

"Jelly beans on toast, I think."

The wise wind whispered,

"Give him time.

Leave him lots of food and drink."

e sniffed the food

and tried to walk,

wobbling around

Izzy and Whizzy.

"He has been out

at sea so long.

Perhaps that's why

he is so *dizzy!*"

eg looked at the puppy
and smiled.

"He has the **legs** of a compass,

a north, south, east and west.

Each one wants to take the lead

and thinks that it knows best."

Puppy tried to run

and chase Kick's favourite stick.

"Oh look out!" cried Quick.

Puppy was very

sick!

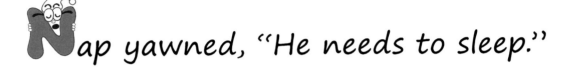ap yawned, "He needs to sleep."

Puppy agreed...

and fell down in a heap.

uppy slept...

and slept...

and slept...

until...

he'd slept enough.

With sleep and food

Puppy got stronger,

so Rising Rhymers all were happy,

but no-one knew where he would wander.

He was their

dizzy-leg-sick chappy!

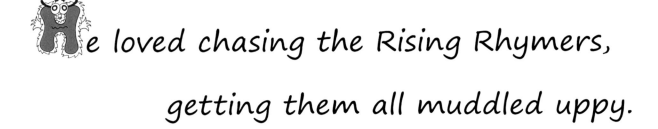e loved chasing the Rising Rhymers,

getting them all muddled uppy.

Then he'd lick them all to show

he liked being their

Mubble Puppy.

The Rhymers & Rising Rhymers – Meet them all

Vroom & Zoom	Pop & Top	Over & Under
Nap & Yap	Mime & Rhyme	Kick & Quick
Izzy & Whizzy	Hairy & Scary	Giggle & Jiggle
Flex & X	Egg & Leg	Crash & Dash
	Ace & Bass	Mubble Pup

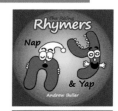

Rhyming alphabet stories
for the capital Rhymers
and little letter Rising Rhymers

Stories for loveable Mubble Pup
and little Mubble Puppy,
The Rhymers' dizzy-leg-sick dog

Early learning books teaching the
alphabet, numbers, colours, shapes
and more

Colouring storybooks
and puzzle books full of mazes,
wordsearches, games and more

Rag Doll Deb
Count

www.meettherhymers.com
www.andrewbuller.com

Made in the USA
Charleston, SC
08 November 2016